The Mistress Under the Hill

An Erotic Horror Short About Bargains

Annabeth Leong

Cover Design by James, GoOnWrite.com

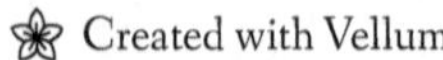

Praise for Annabeth Leong

Annabeth Leong is a mistress of the bittersweet fantasy with the unpredictable conclusion.

— Jean Roberta, author of *Sex Is All Metaphors*

Let's face it, this author is firmly in charge of her pen. She takes imaginative risks that really pay off. She understands the true depths and creativity of sexual connection... including the pain and euphoria it can bring. She tunes deeply into the human spirit and the myths that lie buried in us all. She knows how we struggle and isn't afraid of emotions. She has a very big heart and her imagination is boundless.

— Lana Fox, co-founder, Go Deeper Press

I'll eagerly read anything by Annabeth Leong.

— Lisabet Sarai, author of The Toymakers Guild books

For J. Blackmore, who asked me to write this.

Chapter One

A slit of a window, a bar on the door. A room three paces long, two paces wide. No furniture besides a bed and small dresser, both built by her father. A chamber pot, thank the Lord. Mercy knows these things well, but it is her ritual to check and check them again whenever he locks her in like this.

She opens the curtains and presses her eye to the window. Through the slats attached across the outside, she can just see the path beside the house, and beyond it, the cairn atop the haunted hill. Its white stones gleam in the evening light. The groans from there carry on the wind, reaching Mercy even in her prison of a home. Her spine tingles and her insides itch. She sighs and leans her forehead against the tiny opening to the outside world. A tuft of fresh air blesses her skin.

She waits as long as she can, then paces. Three steps for the length, two for the width. Three steps for the length, two for the width. Her best hope is to wear herself out. Sleep consumes unbearable hours.

For now, she prays. *Sweet Jesus, dear Savior, why did*

God create me beautiful as the devil? Why would He place me on His green earth for no purpose other than tempting men from His commandments? Mercy has barely seen herself, but these are her father's words. He shouts them whenever his fingers close around her upper arm to drag her to this room and shut her in.

She still wears her hat, her going-out clothes. He let her accompany him to the general store today. She should have known better than to accept the offer. People had looked at her there. Her father had seen them lusting after her.

Mercy has often wondered why her father has not given her in marriage, making her someone else's problem. She is long past the age. But seven years ago, her father sent Jeremiah Chittwood away empty-handed, followed by Thomas Parker soon after. Three years ago, he beat Adam Thetcher to a bloody pulp. No one has come to ask for her since.

The sun has yet to dip past the horizon, but Mercy already wants a drink of water. It's useless to pound on the door and beg, but she tries it anyway. She wonders how long before he lets her out. The worst was three days, and she'd been sick for a week after.

She gives up hope and sits on the edge of the bed. Mercy often wonders what it would be like to have a husband. She closes her eyes and passes the time with a familiar game.

"I love you," she whispers.

"And I you." Her own voice, lowered and disguised. Mercy reaches out to the side and clutches the bedspread, imagining fingers, smooth and strong and interlaced with hers. She concentrates as hard as she can on the sensation of skin. It would be warm. She would feel a few hairs from the man's fingers. He might stroke the back of her hand with a callused thumb.

"Shall we go to bed?"

"By all means. I long for you."

Mercy eases the hat off her head, tendrils of her red hair falling down beside her chin. "Why don't you undress me?" She likes the sound of her voice in that sentence, both sweet and coy. She tries it out a few times, a few different ways, tasting the breath of it. "Why don't you undress me? Why don't you undress me?"

Her hands tremble on their way to the top button of her high-necked wool gown. She strokes first beneath her jaw. Her husband would begin by tilting her face up to his. Mercy presses lips to palm, the barest touch. For all her husband's gentleness, she would feel his barely restrained desire for her.

Her hands snap back to her collar, tugging it so the rough fabric scrapes the soft skin of her throat. Mercy undoes the first button, then the second, smoothing the mulberry material out of the way after each. Her fingertips flutter down the side of her neck, teasing. Her heart pounds hard. She pauses, allowing her pulse to surge rhythmically against her fingers.

"Please," Mercy breathes. "Don't stop there."

She struggles to reach the buttons running down the back of her dress. She flops onto the bed, rolling and tangling her skirts between her legs. She would writhe against her husband while he freed her from these clothes. She can't imagine holding still beneath his touch.

Slowly, methodically, one button and one string at a time, Mercy releases her breasts, the pressure of her clothes around her rib cage gradually letting up and then disappearing. The cloth rustles as it slips away, and Mercy maneuvers herself onto her back, her upper half naked and chilly in the lonely room.

Eyes still squeezed shut, she touches her bare skin, prodding delicately at the soft swells of flesh rising from her chest. She weighs her breasts in her hands, guiding them up and down, left and right. She circles her palms lightly over her nipples, the satin skin on the tip of each breast growing rougher as it tightens and hardens to little pointed nubs.

Mercy wishes she could give a face to this husband. She wants to see his concentration as he transforms her this way, his admiration for her beauty, the love in his eyes. But it's not the clerk at the general store she wants, nor Thomas Parker. Jeremiah Chittwood has aged and changed since the days he sought her hand, and she can no longer summon the image of Adam Thetcher without also seeing his swollen eyelids and broken nose. She shakes her head to banish the disturbing memory and lets the man of her daydream remain vague.

"Pinch me," Mercy says, and clamps down on her left nipple, twisting and tugging. The sensation of her own firm grip radiates through her body, tightening her throat and lungs and causing her hips to lift into the air. She crushes it harder between her thumb and the side of her first finger, biting her lip to keep the voice out of her gasps. Mercy tries the other one, drifting her eyes open now to watch the dark pink flesh stretch away from her breast and then snap back into place.

She slaps one palm against each breast sharply enough to sting her taut nipples and waits a beat to make sure she hasn't caught her father's attention. Hearing no sound from the rest of the house, she proceeds to squeeze with all her strength, gritting her teeth to hold in the moan forming in the back of her throat. "I love you," she sighs.

Quickly now, Mercy struggles out of the rest of her clothing, kicking the hump of it away and off the bed. She rests a little, enjoying the ache in her breasts as she tickles the sides of her stomach with her fingers.

Then it is time for her secret discovery. Mercy tries to draw the moment out, feathering touches over her inner thighs and scraping her fingernails across her hips, but she can only hold back so much. Setting her jaw, she imagines her arms around her dream husband. He holds her just as tightly. In her mind, Mercy wraps herself around him in every way she can, as firmly as she can.

Her right hand forms a fist and she slides it to the place between her legs. She nestles her fist against the heat and stickiness and presses there. Her hips find the rhythm on their own, sliding and working against Mercy's hard, round fist, rubbing those soft, humid parts against it. The sensations begin between her legs, but soon spread, extending into her lower belly and down her inner thighs. Mercy's body goes rigid. She points her toes. She grunts softly in the back of her throat.

Her fantasy forgotten, the winding, straining pleasure of the movement drives her on, teaching her what to do and how to move. Finally, Mercy gives a long, loud exhale as the pleasure lifts to a breaking point and pulses through her body. She rolls onto her side with her legs pressed together as tight as a vise around her fist, drinking the feeling down to the dregs.

Mercy pants. A drop of sweat rolls across her hairline. The smell of her body fills the room, and now she hopes her father will take his time releasing her, waiting long enough for some of this pungent odor to dissipate. But it's not an unpleasant scent to her. She relaxes her fist and brings the side of her hand up to her nose, breathing herself in.

She wants water desperately, but the strong smell centers and calms her. It's a way of lingering inside the bursting moment of pleasure, when she has no worries and knows the grace of God. She is safe within her secret discovery, beyond the reach of her father and his strange, strict rules.

Mercy treasures the sensation as her eyes focus and she comes back to herself, sitting up carefully in the bed.

"Lovely," says a voice – a real voice – and Mercy is too frightened even to scream. She snatches her dress from the floor and holds it crumpled against her breasts.

"Well, don't do that," the voice murmurs. It comes from the tiny slits in the window. "Beauty such as yours should remain unbound."

"Who are you?" Mercy manages to stammer.

"Come and see."

She crosses the tiny room, lifting one eye to the largest space between the slats. She and the bearer of the voice would be pressing their faces together if not for the wall between them.

He is flesh and blood, with none of the usual color to sweeten the deal. White flesh, red irises, hair the shade of cobwebs. Short for a man, he strains up onto his toes to reach the window.

But she feels his breath, warm against her upper lip and smelling of the damp world outside the house.

"You needn't fear me," the man tells Mercy. "I have observed without permission, but my transgressions go no further. I require your invitation for all else."

"It's for you I fear," Mercy says. She explains about Adam Thetcher.

"You need fear for me even less than for yourself." He laughs. The sound barely remains on the sane side of madness, the sort of noise that makes one wish the evening light would not leave so soon.

"I owe you a favor, Mercy Broome," he says, and she does not need to ask how he knows her name. "I must make a fair trade for what I took from you."

She smiles doubtfully. "What favor can you give, considering all that separates us?"

"Have you seen a man, Mercy?" When she does not respond, he continues. "Wouldn't you like to?"

His fingers crawl to the buttons of his shirt. Mercy holds her breath. She should stop him, but the pounding still between her legs says she cannot. True, he is not beautiful as Jeremiah Chittwood once was, but where are her pretty suitors now? This man unveils himself before her.

The man uncovers a small, powerful body. Pale, curling hairs start at the base of his neck and thatch his chest. In the dying day, harsh shadows form below his rounded pectoral muscles, almost obscuring his equally chiseled stomach and the stirring dimly visible within his trousers.

The stranger discards his clothes on the ground outside Mercy's window without a care, never taking his piercing, predatory eyes from her face. He runs the flats of his hands down his sides, defining his shape for her. Below his stout chest, his waist seems narrow as a girl's, but his thighs sprout thick as young trees.

Her eyes follow the movements of his fingertips. He smiles knowingly and toys with her gaze. Now coy, he displays the layers of scars at the points of his elbows. Now lewd, he cups the heavy sack that hangs between his legs, lifting and stroking it for her. Hanging before it, his hardening cock. She notes the blunt head, its slitted eye, the thick pink stalk. With dramatic gestures, the man draws it out, lengthening it and bringing it to life before Mercy's eyes.

Her fingers shake, wound in the lattice of slats over the

window in an unconscious effort to get closer, to touch as well as look.

He grins as if reading her and spits on the palm of his hand. Rubbing and polishing the knob at the end of his pole of flesh, the stranger breaks gaze with Mercy for the first time, his eyelids falling closed. A wrinkle forms on the bridge of his nose, and she recognizes his need to concentrate on pleasure, budding and burgeoning.

The man's free hand extends, the fingers curled into a strange, spasmodic position. The other wraps fully around his cock, the tease fading from his movements, replaced by focus.

Mercy's curious eyes devour him. His head sinks low in his pleasure, taut shoulders hunched up around his ears, the muscles cording in his neck. He rocks his hips into his hand, rises onto his toes, breathes heavily through his nose. The tip of his tongue, alarmingly red, just breaks the seal of his lips at the left corner, twitching slightly as he jerks himself.

Then his mouth pops open with one ragged moan. Thick white cords of fluid spurt from the tip of his cock, arcing from his body in a series of pulses.

Slowly, he opens his eyes, holding up one messy hand for her inspection. Mercy squirms on her side of the wall, locked away by the window and her father's control. She pokes her nose out through the opening and he understands, bringing his hand close enough for her to smell. The salt of air blown west from the sea floods Mercy's senses. For a moment, she can remember the sun breaking from the constant gray above.

Mercy hesitates, then flicks out her tongue, just grazing the tip against the sticky fluid on his hand. Withdrawing to her mouth, she savors the speck of flavor, thick and bitter.

Not a child's flavor. Mercy tastes the woman's life she has been denied.

"Lovely," the stranger says again. He remains naked. Mercy slowly lets fall the clump of clothes she's been holding against herself. Longing bursts through her, centered in the depths of her stomach, but radiating far beyond.

The stranger's gaze feels like fingers, stroking her everywhere. Mercy sighs aloud.

"Come with me," the man says. "Be my bride, the mistress under the hill. I will do anything you ask."

His gaze shifts. He squints. Mercy glances over her shoulder, following his eyes. She can't see through walls, but she knows in her gut that he's staring directly at her father. She shivers. The stranger steps closer to the window. All she sees now are his red, blood-filled lips. "Anything you ask," he repeats.

She wants. She dreams. She cannot.

Mercy leaps forward and draws the curtains closed. She sits on the bed, hands wrapping her chest, gasping until she's sure the stranger has moved on.

Chapter Two

A brow twisted as wind-battered trees looms above Mercy. Her father's fierce blue left eye glares down at her, measuring and disapproving. The other eye, made of glass, simply stares. He slaps her cheek, the sting light. He's not really angry at her.

"Dress yourself properly, girl."

Mercy clears her dry throat, stretches her cracked lips. She crawled into her clothes after the stranger left, but her skirts are tangled now from hours of tossing in her bed, feverish and thirsty. She pulls herself back from her father, wrapping herself in a ball in the shadow of the bed's headboard. She nods.

"You look like a horror," he says.

"I'm sorry." Her voice sounds unfamiliar.

"Goody Keyne will come to dinner tonight. You've a lot to do to get the house ready."

Mercy can't speak any more. She stands to show her readiness, all too aware of every wrinkle in every dress and the stench of her unwashed body. She lurches, dizzy from her head's rapid change in elevation. Her father studies her, sneers, and leaves the room.

Chapter Three

Goody Keyne talks endlessly of the gospels, but she never gives her opinion on anything in them. Mercy sits patiently through her rendition of the Sermon on the Mount, and then a description of the thoughts of many preachers on the subject. Mercy's father praises the old woman for her memory, her fine choice of words, and her devotion.

Mercy sips her drink as slowly as she can manage, not wanting to call attention to the raging thirst she still feels. She knows from experience that it will take a few days for it to pass, unless she wishes to risk being accused of gluttony in order to slake it.

When her father at last sees Goody Keyne to the door, Mercy allows herself to deflate. She retreats to her room and shuts herself in, only then noticing the fine gown spread over her bed.

It shimmers against the dull brown of her bedclothes. Blue as the late evening sky! Mercy has never seen such a color. It must surely be vanity, and yet she cannot stop herself from touching the fabric, the weave more perfect than anything she could achieve, the thread spun more delicately.

Mercy lifts the dress and hugs it against her chest. Goosebumps rise everywhere the soft fabric touches. Unknown perfume wafts from the material, the expensive scent of a flower too exotic for Mercy to recognize.

Her heart pounding, she undoes her own plain, high-necked dress and replaces it with this new, elegant garment. She smooths it over her body. The gown transforms her touch. She gives a powerful shiver. She need not ask herself from whence it came – only one source could explain such a gift.

Mercy experiments, spinning in a circle on the small patch of bare floor in her bedroom. Unsatisfied desire crystallizes in her chest, presenting an image of one compelling transgression.

She does not dare, and yet cannot resist. Before she has time to question herself, Mercy unfastens her bedroom door. She treads lightly as a ghost, and yet the wooden floor still creaks beneath her step. Cringing with every movement, Mercy creeps through the house, where she eases the front door open and steals out.

None of her shoes can reach the level of the gown she wears, and so Mercy walks barefoot. The haunted hill pulls at her bones. She could travel there without looking or thinking.

The night sings with mysteries that Mercy has always been denied. Gentle buzzes, flashes of unexplained light, and whispering leaves signal that Mercy's secrets will easily blend with the many others that together weave the thick blanket of darkness.

Moist ground kisses the soles of her feet with each step she takes. The smell of earth enfolds her. Moonlight caresses her. Mercy knows he is waiting for her at the hill. Her pace speeds at the thought of him, his pale eyelids blinking over blood-colored eyes. His eyes like wounds, open to the sight of her.

She nears the hill. Pebbles bruise the bottoms of her feet, forcing her into an awkward dance along the path. And music bursts into the night, plunging Mercy into a dance indeed. Apparitions around her twist their bodies into graceful, broken forms, glimpsed from the corner of an eye, perceived by the hairs on the back of the neck.

Mercy rises onto her toes and moves faster still, the beat of the music accelerating with her. Her head spins with the confusion of the movement flashing around her. Her mind can't grasp her surroundings. She glances back toward the house but can't see it through the viscous dark.

Then a hand in hers. "If I may?"

She smiles at him. Their fingers interlace. He guides her into the dance completely, the subtle pressure of his fingers somehow teaching Mercy's feet where to fall. The shapes around her change and clarify. Women in jewel-encrusted gowns. Men in shoes that shine like the moon. But all remain strange – too tall, too thin, too pale, or too dark.

Mercy knows she doesn't belong among these creatures, but then her stranger slides one hand down to the curve of her waist and she relinquishes her fears to the strength of his grip.

"Do you have a name?" Mercy breathes.

"Samuel."

They dance for hours, until Mercy's feet bleed and her knees quiver. Still, she does not want to stop. Samuel senses her weakness, supporting her weight and drawing her closer to him.

"The night will be over soon," he whispers. Mercy

shakes her head in disbelief. They dance alone. She did not notice the other creatures retreating, did not see the moon fading before the coming dawn.

"Will you keep the dress and be my bride?" His lips smile against her ear. "Or will you return the gift to me now?"

Mercy freezes in his arms. "Now?"

"Oh, yes. Something of yours must remain at my hill in exchange for what I sacrificed." He grips her hips tightly. "Let it be you. My mistress under the hill. And ask what you will." Again, that significant glance, into the distance this time. Mercy holds no doubt – he stares directly at her father.

Mercy pulls back and is a little surprised when Samuel lets her go. She hesitates, lifting her fingers to the buttons of the dress but not following through.

"Look at what I did for you," he says. He loosens his own clothes. The marks of teeth purple at his throat. Angry, scabbed scratches mar the sides of his arms, his chest, and his back. The wounds seem to writhe against the canvas of his colorless skin.

"I don't understand."

He steps free of his trousers, his cock a tall, hard cylinder standing out from his body. "Take off the dress."

Mercy shivers and obeys. She peels the sweat-stained dress away from her skin, its expensive scent mingled now with the smell of her own body.

"Look at it," Samuel says.

Mercy glances down, at the wrong side of the fabric. Stains she hadn't noticed bloom across its surface, sticky and fresh. "What did—?"

"Its owner did not give it over easily."

The implications of the rusty color marring the inside of

the dress sink in. Mercy screams and thrusts the garment out at arm's length, paying no mind to the chill pre-dawn air playing over her naked body.

Samuel steps closer. She recognizes the smell of his cock. The red of his eyes deepens, mirroring the stains on the dress. "I want to give you what you wish for most of all," he whispers. "Anything you ask. I want to serve you. Please. I need to."

Mercy vibrates with longing. She cannot release her grip on the beautiful dress. Neither can she step back from him.

He lifts a hand toward her face. She waits, but he refrains from contact.

"I can only touch with your permission," he reminds her.

Mercy draws in a shaky breath. Before she can change her mind, she jerks forward, pressing her cheek into his palm. He groans.

"I won't stay," she says quickly. "And I won't keep the dress. But..." She trails one finger over the half-open cuts on his throat. He sucks in a lungful of air. Mercy leans nearer. The tiny hairs on his neck move in response to the rhythm of her exhalations. "I thank you. For everything. For... giving me something fine, wherever it came from. For making me feel pretty." Squeezing her eyes shut, she kisses the wound, rubbing her soft lips across its scabby, ragged edges.

When she pulls back, he's gritting his teeth, both hands fisted at his sides. "What's wrong?"

"Do you think it's easy to follow the rules that separate us?"

Mercy smiles. All her life, her father has warned her about men and their uncontrollable passions, and this is the first time she has been free enough to gather any clue of what he means.

She knows she cannot accept Samuel's offer, even if he is the only man who stands a chance of getting her away from her father. Lord knows what manner of creature he is. Still, she wants him. She notices the dress, clutched forgotten in her extended fist. She lifts it to her face, allowing it to unfurl. It snaps softly in the wind that rushes over the hill.

Mercy takes one of Samuel's hands, forcing the fingers open. His restraint thrills her, a triumph over the lust that vibrates between their naked bodies. Mercy wraps his hand with the stained dress, then releases him.

"Touch me," she whispers, "but only through the dress."

He hisses. She trembles so hard her teeth chatter. Mercy locks her fingers together behind her back to keep from inadvertently resisting.

The soft fabric kisses her throat, but she knows the light touch is only a prelude. Next, he engulfs her right breast in a harsh grip, tugging her so close his breath heats her face and his lips hover just over her cheek. She wonders if he will break her restriction with a kiss, but he does not. He holds her on the razor's edge of it, squeezing her breast ever tighter.

Mercy's head spins. She barely remembers to breathe. He shifts to her nipple, the dress seeming rough now compared to that soft skin. It hurts, but it also makes her ache.

She meets his eyes and grabs his wrist, guides his hand down between her legs. The wad of the garment presses against her most sensitive place, backed by his firm hold. Mercy braces her hands on his shoulders and grinds her hips to please herself.

Samuel holds steady, maintaining even pressure for her to buck against. Mercy's juices wet the fabric, softening the sensation as she rubs it. She adds another stain to it, willingly.

It is hard to keep her eyes on Samuel. She wants to slip into her private world of fantasy, the place where she has always been safe. But she resists. She wants to bring him into her, and so she keeps her eyes open to him, imagining that he can see through them to the images that run through her head.

She pictures his mouth covering one breast and then the other, biting and kissing, confusing pain and pleasure. She would spread herself for him but tremble, wanting and fearing him, never certain if his next touch will bring kindness or cruelty.

Standing before her, Samuel smiles slightly. As if he knows. She shivers at the idea of him entering her mind. It's so close to the other forbidden thought she has – of his cock thrusting into her body. Mercy presses the side of her face against his, breathing in the damp earth aroma that rises from his chilly, pale skin. She sighs and comes, shuddering against his cloth-covered hand.

His limbs stay in place, but air charges in and out of his lungs. Against her cheek, his jaw shifts. He grinds his teeth, a soft growl rising in the back of his throat. "If you will leave me tonight, let it be now," he says.

Still feeling the clenching glow of her release, Mercy pulls back. Water in the eyes belies Samuel's fierce expression. She feels a rush of affection that frightens her more than the idea of what he did to get the dress.

The early call of a bird reminds her that dawn will break any moment, and she is naked. Mercy nods once to Samuel and flees toward her house as if the devil himself pursues her. She wonders if he does.

Chapter Four

The house seems to sleep. Mercy creeps closer with increasing trepidation. She knows how she looks.

Though she is barefoot, she makes noise every step. Twigs crack, or Mercy hisses in pain as a stone presses up into the wounds on her soles. It's more light than dark by now, and every second brings more of the sun's blaze.

She steals to the front door, wincing at the creaking of the half-rotten outside stairs. She can guide it open silently, she tells herself, and race to her room and climb into her bed before her father is the wiser.

Holding her breath, she tries it, as slowly and carefully as a stalking woodsman. She takes her time. Not a sound escapes from the big, wooden door. Mercy smiles to herself and enters the house.

"Whore!"

She flinches and shrinks back, but her father yanks her inside and slams the door. His seeing eye squints but the skin around his glass eye can't mirror the expression. He glares lopsided and monstrous at Mercy's bleeding feet and exposed body.

"All these years," he whispers. "I feared for you. I protected you. And how do you treat me now?"

Mercy lifts her chin. She has never talked back to him, but words burn inside her throat. "You hurt people who had committed no sin against me or you." Adam Thetcher. Had she loved him? It is impossible to say now – the thought of him brings so much guilt.

"Were you the sinner, then? I knew it from your youth. I gave life to a Delilah." He touches her hair for a moment, but snatches his hand back as if seared. "Red hair and green eyes. The devil's blood must have come from your mother's line." He covers his face with both hands. "And a shape that would destroy a man!" He stumbles away from the door. "Go to your room!" he screams.

Mercy hangs her head, intending to obey, but she cannot bring herself to move. It's not been a full day since her last stint locked up and starving. She hasn't the strength or the will.

"Go! Now!"

"No," Mercy whispers.

"What?"

"No." Her voice strengthens. "You will not confine me again. I have done no wrong."

For a moment, she questions herself. Has not her behavior with Samuel been thoroughly wicked? And yet the thought holds no force for Mercy. She has long wished for matrimony. She dreamed for years of sharing herself with a husband. But her father has punished her with one hand for not taking the path he denies her with the other. No. Mercy will please herself from now on, without apology.

She stands tall and faces her father. He stares as if he

doesn't know her. She can't look away from his glass eye, so wide and unfeeling, holding no sympathy for her at all.

She knows what he will do a moment before the first blow strikes, and braces herself as best she can. Not good enough. Mercy falls to the floor. She curls into a ball. The beating continues with heavy, dull strikes along her spine. Mercy tries to crawl away. No escape.

Chapter Five

She throbs into consciousness. The bed she lies in hurts. The light of the sun hurts. Breathing hurts. Being awake inside her body hurts. She opens her eyes, wailing at the familiar sight. A faint glow through the slit of a window. A bar on the door. The dull, familiar ceiling. The bed, the dresser, and the spot of floor.

She is thirsty already. Mercy sits up, gasps at the pain in her head, and drops back down.

"I have a gift for you," a familiar voice says, from inside the room this time. Mercy gives a little scream and gets up despite her body's protests. Her father must have dressed her before putting her to bed, and the stiff, plentiful fabric that covers and chokes her bruised skin creates pain in its own right.

"Samuel?" He is shadowed in the corner, sitting like a little boy with his knees drawn up under his chin. He regards her with eyes that appear all the more bloody considering his haggard face.

"It is the best gift I could find." He opens a hand, holding it out to Mercy. On his palm sits a finger, adorned with a fine ruby ring. Mercy knows that she should ask where this has come from, but he looks so distressed that she forgets even her own pain and kneels on the floor before him, one hand stroking his white hair.

"What happened to you?"

He is shaking. He thrusts his open palm at her more insistently. "Take the gift and make the trade. Come with me to be mistress under the hill." He shuts his eyes, the accusation in his voice aimed in all directions. "You should not have left when last we met. You should not have."

Mercy peers at the finger in his hand. Diamonds swirl around the ruby. Someone lovingly carved an inscription in the gold of the ring: "Autre ne veut." She frowns at the foreign words. She wrinkles her nose at the smell of the lady's finger. Mercy does not want to think about this.

Gently, she lifts the finger from his hand and sets it beside him on the floor. "How did you get inside?"

"I had to be near you. Even if I could not help you." He glares at his hands, clenching and unclenching them.

"Why?"

"How many times must I ask you to be my bride? Do you not understand my feelings? I will do anything you ask, and yet you do not ask." This time, he does not look beyond her. He keeps his eyes on her, and his meaning remains crystal clear.

Mercy shudders. He transforms the aching of her body from pain to longing. She leans forward slowly, her bruises twinging despite her care. She guides her lips to his and waits there. Neither one moves for a while. They hold their pose, breathing each other's breath.

Then her mouth parts, but he will take nothing without explicit permission, and so Mercy presses her tongue through his lips instead. He tastes of blood and dirt and secrets. She moans and kisses harder, beginning to crawl into his lap until she leans her weight on a fearsome bruise and breaks off with a yelp.

She crumples beside him, panting, with tears in her eyes. "I need you to touch me," she whispers. "Please."

She sets no conditions. In the depths of her despair, she cares nothing for her virtue. She has heard that a woman suffers in her first congress with a man, but what pain could Samuel cause her that she does not already feel? She abandons herself to his arms, preparing for his invasion.

He does not ravish her. He lifts her off the floor and carries her to the bed, but when they get there he only strokes her hair.

"I love you," she whispers. It does not matter if it is true.

"And I you." His thumb rubs circles on the back of her hand, softer than her own skin, and cold.

"Why don't you undress me?"

Silence thickens the room, and then his hands tremble their way to the top button of her high-necked wool gown. He stops before unfastening it. One palm runs down the side of her face, just grazing her. She turns to kiss his palm. For all his gentleness, his barely restrained desire burns there beneath her lips, and his anger.

"Please," Mercy breathes. "Don't stop there."

His hands snap back to her collar, tugging it so the rough fabric scrapes the soft skin of her throat. The first button gives way to his pull, then the second. His fingertips flutter down the side of her neck, and he pricks her with hints of his sharp nails. Her heart pounds. He freezes. Her pulse surges rhythmically against his fingers.

Mercy can't hold still beneath his touch. She writhes against Samuel, tangling herself further in the dress, despite her need to be released. Cold, unnaturally smooth lips light against her throat. "Be still," he says.

She obeys, closing her eyes as he peels the dress from her. She sighs as her breasts and ribs come free, and then her stomach. Relieved of the garment's constriction, the thudding pain of her bruises eases.

Cloth whispers above her, and then the wiry hair on his chest rubs against the tender skin of hers. He flings an arm over her, their bodies slightly tacky where they make contact. Mercy smiles and reaches for him, but he is not where she expects.

His lips journey down her body, walking the length of the hard bone between her breasts. He continues, letting her stomach pillow his kisses. He nudges her thighs apart.

The first tap of his tongue against the secret center of her pleasure jerks Mercy nearly upright. Samuel murmurs soothingly, then puts tongue to her again, slower this time. His tongue travels firm and luxurious through the cleft between her legs, coaxing folds of skin apart with barely any pressure at all. Its touch flickers. It could almost be one of Mercy's fantasies, except that she has never imagined such a thing before.

Carefully, as if she might bolt, Samuel's hands wrap around her thighs, holding her in place. He increases the force of his tongue, licking faster now. Three upward strokes, two across, and back again. The regularity of the pleasure lulls and relaxes Mercy. His tongue paces her body the way she used to pace this little bedroom. Its rhythm tells her she has plenty of time.

She gazes at the ceiling and allows him to conduct her at his own pace toward the point of release. Can she truly share this refuge with another? Mercy arches up toward his tongue. Her legs strain but she does not rock the way she wants to.

Samuel's right hand creeps higher up her thigh. He swipes a finger through the liquid pooling between her legs. He runs the tip of his finger around Mercy's opening and presses his tongue flat against her body.

Pleasure bursts like a bubble. She grips the back of his head and holds him tight against her. Mercy wishes the world could stop then and there, leaving her frozen in that mind-erasing moment.

Samuel remains patiently in place until she releases him. He lifts his head, his chin glistening with her juices. Mercy leans down and strokes her finger under his lip, gathering up her own wetness. Bringing her hand to her nose, she closes her eyes and breathes her own scent, mingled with the graveyard flavor of Samuel's mouth.

He crawls up her body, his cock hard between them. She meets his strange, red eyes. "What gift will you accept?" Samuel whispers. "In exchange for becoming mistress under the hill?"

Mercy swallows hard. She spreads her legs wide around him. She twists her face to the side, as if she is the one who can see through walls. "One glass eye," she tells him quickly. She turns back in time to see his smile, just before he plunges himself into her waiting body.

Author's Note

I wrote "The Mistress Under the Hill" at the request of J. Blackmore, who was putting together Circlet Press's very first horror anthology, invitation-only. Circlet Press has always had a commitment to sex positivity, and publisher Cecilia Tan had some concerns about erotic horror as it often appears – namely, that the sexual content in erotic horror is often more horrifying than erotic, and relatedly, that it often sends moralistic messages about the sick, twisted nature of sex.

I wonder now if those concerns influenced the way I wrote the character of Mercy's father – a man so horrified by the erotic that he himself becomes a horror and drives his daughter into the arms of a horror in the process.

This was the pitch I sent in response to the invitation:

"I'm interested in doing a voyeur story. My current thought is that a woman notices a man watching her undress and gradually starts performing for him in exchange for increasingly creepy favors. I'm always interested in the addictive quality of going to extremes, and I plan to bring the horror element in by having her continue getting a sexual thrill out of the relationship long after it's clear that he's a malevolent spirit and that what they're doing is steadily corrupting her. I'm planning to address the concerns about sex positivity by locating most of the horror in what she gets from him in exchange, rather than in the sex act itself. However, I do think that the exchange is part of what she finds exciting."

What interests me years later is how the story evolved from the idea in the pitch. For example, the setting, which feels integral when I read the story now, doesn't exist at all in the original idea.

Another thing that evolved is the sweetness. The pitch seems to describe a gritty, cynical story, but to me "The Mistress Under the Hill" is, perhaps disturbingly, sweet and romantic. By the time I get to the end, I want Mercy and Samuel to wind up together, the same way I want the main characters to end up together when I read a Harlequin romance.

In the introduction to *What Lies Beneath: Erotic Horror*, where the story was originally published, J. Blackmore described Mercy as having to choose which evil she wants to belong to. I can't deny that Samuel is evil – he not only seems to be murdering for Mercy's gifts, but also has an unmistakable taste for the act. However, in the final scene, my heart goes out to them both. They strike me as broken children who grew into broken adults seeking some sort of love, healing, acceptance and peace from each other.

This has always been one of my favorites among my stories, and the lingering horror for me comes from realizing which side I'm on. Like Mercy, I don't really care where that finger came from.

Author's Note

I revisited this story as part of putting together my collection *Dark, Trembling Passion: Erotic Horror Shorts*. If you enjoyed "The Mistress Under the Hill," I'd really appreciate you picking up the full collection.

• *Annabeth Leong, January* 2022

Acknowledgments

This story would not exist without J. Blackmore, who commissioned it for Circlet Press's first erotic horror anthology, *What Lies Beneath.*

Looking through correspondence around the creation of that book, I felt how deeply influenced I have been by so many people in the orbit of Circlet, including Cecilia Tan, who started it all; Bethany Zaiatz, a snappy dresser who always understood what people were excited to read; and Elizabeth Schechter, who came up with the theme of "Haunted" to guide the book. The other authors who took part in *What Lies Beneath* deserve recognition: Bernie Mojzes, A.C. Wise, Lucy A. Snyder, Kaysee Renee Robichaud, and Kannan Feng – you should look for all their work because they are amazing writers. I also want to thank Nobilis Reed, who created an audio version of "The Mistress Under the Hill" for the Nobilis Erotica podcast and later included it in *Like a Whisper in Your Ear: Aural Erotic Science Fiction.*

I have a bit of a bittersweet feeling because it seems like the world has changed since we put that erotic horror book together. However, I want to avoid giving in to the idea that the golden age lies in the past. I thank and acknowledge any reader of this story, whether you found it in one of its original venues or are just discovering it now.

About the Author

Annabeth Leong's writing has been recognized in a long list of best-of anthologies, including *Heiresses of Russ 2015: The Year's Best Lesbian Speculative Fiction*, *Best Women's Erotica 2015*, *Best Women's Erotica of the Year Volume 2*, *The Very Best of House of Erotica Volume One*, and several editions of *Best Lesbian Erotica*, *Best Erotic Romance*, *Best Bondage Erotica* and more.

When Circlet Press put together *Superlative Speculative Erotica: The Best of Circlet Press 2012-2017*, they asked campaign contributors to vote on which stories to include. Annabeth was the overall top vote-getter, and had the most stories make the top ten list.

Annabeth's work is always erotic, frequently speculative and often queer, though she isn't afraid to write heterosexual erotic romance set in the modern world.

Both the author and her writing can be slippery at times, drawn to exploring forbidden territory and making exquisite mistakes.

AEL Publishing recently began releasing new editions of Annabeth Leong's work, including some titles that have never before been seen.

Also by Annabeth Leong

From AEL Publishing

Erotic Horror

Dark, Trembling Passion: Erotic Horror Shorts

Contemporary Erotic Romance Novels

Renovations

The Fugitive's Sexy Brother

Lesbian Short Fiction

If Looks Could Kink: 3 Erotic F/F Stories of Femmes on Top

www.ingramcontent.com/pod-product-compliance
Lightning Source LLC
LaVergne TN
LVHW020532160826
845677LV00015B/4009
9798420819883